Rabbits and Spiders

Peter Marney

ISBN-13: 978-1976374579
ISBN-10: 197637457X

This book is dedicated to
daydreamers everywhere.

Read this first

You are not a ninja.

It's very important that you know this fact.

It's very important because if you try to copy any of the stuff in this book then you might end up getting hurt or getting into trouble.

This will be bad.

This will be very bad because I'll get the blame.

So please, remember you're not a ninja and promise not to copy any of this stuff.

Have you promised?

Ok, you can now read on.

Blind date

I've decided to murder Red.

Something slow and painful I think, or maybe just very bloody. She deserves it.

I'm Jamie by the way and Red used to be my best friend before I decided to kill her.

Why?

Because she deserves it! And she deserves it because I'm having to sit through this stupid film in the dark and avoid holding hands with Dog Girl.

“Come on Jamie, you know you like films and besides, it’ll be fun.”

No Red, it won’t.

“You know Tammy’s upset at the moment so we’re just being good friends and looking after her.”

I’m not convinced.

“I’ll buy you a chocolate milkshake.”

Which is why I’m now sitting in the dark and getting very angry at Red for setting me up on a blind date with Dog Girl and then not turning up herself.

Actually, the film isn’t too bad and I might even enjoy it if Tammy’s head wasn’t snuggling into my shoulder. Red is supposed to protect me from all this stuff, not land me right in the middle of it.

In case you’re wondering why we’re not at school, it’s a Saturday.

Normally I'd be at home in our flat helping Red and Naz, my other friend, do our usual chores and get our washing done while Kiera, who's sort of our temporary mother, does the food shopping.

Naz is also friends with Dog Girl which is why Tammy was sleeping over last night and why I've got landed with her. Oh, and by the way, she fancies me according to Red who knows about these sort of things.

I suppose I should also mention the toothache which kept Naz awake for most of the night and which has now sent her and Keira to the emergency dentist leaving me and Red to look after Dog Girl.

Correction; leaving me to look after Dog Girl!

I am so going to kill Red just as soon as this film is finished and I can get home.

Except that isn't what happens which is why I'm now jogging

through the town centre. Red has gone missing and we're out looking for her. Keira is scouting near to our flat and her brother Jack is driving round in circles on the outskirts of the town doing the same thing.

Red is not where she's supposed to be and none of us know why.

Yes, the sensible thing would be to go to the police but that's not a good idea when you're supposed to be in hiding, which is a sort of secret known only to the Red Sock Ninja Clan, which is another secret.

About two hundred years ago, we got into trouble with some very nasty people who would just love to know exactly where we are right now. It's too long a story to go into at the moment but basically, we just can't go to the police.

Instead we're looking for Red ourselves and asking any friends we meet whether they've seen her today, which so far has only brought me a forest of shaking heads. Not good news except it now means that other eyes are also on the lookout.

I'm now searching Red's favourite shops which is where I bump into Miss G, our dance teacher from school. That's what happens when you're not looking where you're going.

"Sorry Miss. Have you seen Red?"

"Do you mean Kate, Jay?"

Oops, I've forgotten to use our hiding names.

"Yes, sorry Miss, that's my nickname for her, because of the red hair?"

Miss G smiles. She does that a lot which is why she's our favourite teacher.

"Yes Jay, I think I can work that out for myself and yes, I did see her earlier."

Earlier turns out to be about ten minutes before she was supposed to meet me and Dog Girl at the cinema.

"She was chatting to a man down by the library. Big chap in a blue suit."

Red doesn't know any men in blue suits.

"I'm not sure if she saw me though because she didn't wave or anything. Almost wasn't sure it was her until she took off her hat and shook out her hair."

My heart stops beating.

It's one of Red's secret signs and it means danger. Red's in trouble. She's missing and she's in trouble.

I try to keep a smile on my face and thank Miss, telling her we'll see her on Monday which is now a lifetime away. I need to find Keira but I also need to find Red.

I say goodbye to Miss and stroll away so as not to look suspicious before breaking into a sprint to get to the library as quickly as possible. Then I start running in circles, ever expanding circles, as I try to cover all of the streets surrounding where Red was last seen. I don't even know what I'm looking for but I've got to do something. Red is my best friend and she's in danger.

Suddenly I see what I should have been looking for.

A public telephone.

Now I can call Keira and give her the news.

Yes, it would be simpler if I had my own mobile and I've been saying that to Keira for months and months but without success. Red has a mobile so why can't I have one? I suppose it doesn't help that Naz hasn't got one either and doesn't want one.

I start dialling the number but hang up before I finish. Something's not right. My mind's trying to tell me something but I've not been listening and now I need to stop flapping about like a wet blondie and open my ears.

It's a trick Keira taught us all a while back. If you get in a flap, stop, take a slow deep breath and start listening to your heartbeat, slowing your breathing until you're calm again. The blood is thundering through my ears at the moment so hearing my heartbeat isn't a problem although slowing my breathing takes rather longer than usual.

What am I missing?

I met Miss, I found out about Red, and I started running. I stopped to call Keira and then I stopped doing that because of what? Why did I stop? What was I thinking about which made me stop?

Mobile!

Red's got a mobile.

I start to dial her number but again stop myself.

If she's in trouble then she'd use the mobile herself. If she hasn't used it then the last thing she needs is it going off and alerting Mister Blue Suit that she's got it tucked away in her bag.

I phone Keira and blurt out my news, then have to do it all again but slower.

Red's in trouble and there's absolutely nothing I can do to help her!

Peter Marney

Find my phone

Naz is still feeling sore after the dentist but at least she's got rid of Dog Girl who's been sent to search near to our school. Tammy doesn't understand the seriousness of the situation and thinks Red's just gone off for a sulk over something or other.

Meanwhile the Red Sock Ninjas sit down and decide what we really know.

One, Red didn't turn up to the film and hasn't been seen since, except by Miss G who saw her talking to a man in a blue suit near the library.

Two, she gave a secret signal warning of danger.

Three; there is no three.

We don't know that Red's been kidnapped by the blue suit but, if he was just some tourist looking for directions, why would she give the sign for danger?

Maybe she just wanted to shake out her hair and it was a coincidence.

"Maybe we should just call her mobile after all and see where she is," I suggest, having run out of any decent ideas.

Naz suddenly gives me a gigantic hug.

"Jamie, that's brilliant! All we need to do is find her phone!"

She explains that when Red was trying to convince her how cool mobiles were, she showed Naz an app which can find your phone when it gets lost. I wish I'd got that app too as the conversation has suddenly gone all tekky and I'm completely lost. Keira and Naz are babbling away in computer speak and have hauled out Red's laptop. For once Keira doesn't have to crack a password as Naz already knows it and soon we're looking at a map of our town with a green pulsing light showing where Red, or at least her phone, is right this very moment.

Keira then switches to another program and pulls up a satellite version of the same map which show us a row of normal houses down a side street off of the main road into town. At the same time, she's calling her brother Jack who will now go and park his car somewhere nearby and keep an eye on the house in question until we can get there.

Keira takes command and starts issuing instructions.

"Naz, I don't want you running around still drugged up and with a sore mouth. Your role is co-ordinator and I want you with Jack when we get there. If Red gets moved then you'll both follow in the car and keep us up to date."

Keira's assuming enemy action and acting accordingly. Naz wants to be more involved but it makes sense not to risk her if she's not up to it today.

"Jamie, see how the garden backs onto the park?"

She points at the map and I follow her finger tracing the path from the park gate to the back of the house.

"I want you there with these."

She hands me a small pair of binoculars.

"I was going to save this for your birthday but I guess we can't wait."

She hands me another box which contains a mobile. My very own mobile!

I want to do a happy dance but it will have to wait. Keira is showing me how to speed dial her and also how to contact Jack. I then quickly get changed into semi ninja gear and we're off. Naz calls Dog Girl on the way and tells her to go home as we've found Red and will explain everything tomorrow which is a sort of hopeful lie.

In the back of the car I play with my phone and take a quick selfie before Keira tells me to put it way. She then drops me at the park gates and heads off to deposit Naz close to Jack's car. She's going to park at the other end of the road and do a couple of walk-bys to see what's going on.

Have you ever seen a cartoon where Hero Mouse or Evil Emu has to climb a tree?

No problem. Straight up the usefully low hanging branch and then right to the top without a hitch. That's how it's done, right?

This isn't a cartoon tree. It doesn't have any low hanging branches or useful footholds for the young tree climber and all I can do is stare up at it. Maybe I should have brought a ladder.

I can't even tell if I've got the right house as most of the houses have fences at the bottom of their gardens blocking the view.

Then my pocket starts vibrating and I nearly wet myself.

I'd forgotten that Keira had switched my new phone to silent mode and it's now telling me in the only way possible that I've got a call.

"In position?"

No names and minimum information just in case someone is listening.

I tell Keira I'm not sure and then have to go to the end of the block and count houses until I reach the right one.

It doesn't make a difference. I still can't see over the fence.

But I do have an idea which is why a tearful Naz is now in the next door garden and looking for my bag which I threw over a few minutes ago. I can hear her talking as she searches.

"It's a black backpack. Two boys stole it from me and then threw it over the fence before running away."

The house owner is a very sympathetic young mum and is helping Naz by the sound of it.

I don't run away but just stroll back the way I came in and go off to find Keira. By the time I get there Naz has found her bag and is reporting back with what else she's found out.

"If the houses are all the same then it's got stairs near the front door and a passageway to the kitchen at the back and the garden. One big front room with the kitchen behind and then a sort of utility room off to one side. That's an add on I think as it's only single storey."

Naz knows how to look. She also knows how to chat to people and ask innocent questions about bedrooms and babies and all that stuff. That's how we know the house layout upstairs as well.

Most people might stop there but Naz also tells us about the types of doors and windows and more importantly, locks. Secret ninjas notice that sort of thing.

If the house next door has the same standard locks then we have a way in.

All we need now is a foolproof rescue plan.

Illegal

Just so we're clear about this, what we do next is very illegal and very wrong. If your friend goes missing, you call the police. You do not try to break into the house yourself and risk the police coming to arrest you instead.

You also don't go walking up the path to knock on the front door. That's a very bad idea unless you're Jack and know how to take care of yourself in a fight. Not that he wants to get in a fight of course.

All he wants to do is tell whoever owns the house about the work he's been doing a few doors up and the dry rot he found. Obviously he'd like the job of sorting it out if this house has the same problem but, as it's potentially dangerous, he felt he should just tell people and let them decide for themselves once they see the rotting bits.

I'd believe him, wouldn't you? He's even speaking like his English isn't too good which makes everything take longer.

Meanwhile, me and Keira have scaled the fence at the bottom of the garden and are now climbing up onto the roof of the extension. I've done this before and it's not as easy as it sounds. The locks on the windows have been changed as well just to make things even more interesting. I'd like to test my lock picking skills but Keira has other ideas. From one of her many pockets she pulls out some sticky stuff and what looks like a pen.

My pocket vibrates again and this time it's Naz. I think she must be using Jack's mobile.

"Confirmed sighting. It's my old church friend."

What?!

This is terrible news. Somehow our enemies have found us and Red's been kidnapped by their boss who we've met before. This could get very dangerous very quickly.

I tell Keira the news and watch as she hesitates, weighing up whether to go ahead with the rescue plan and put all of us in danger, or else retreat and leave Red.

Quickly she draws a circle in the glass and quietly punches it out before reaching in and opening the window. If I didn't know any better

I'd say our Keira was a house burglar in a previous job.

Actually I don't know better and she might well have been a master criminal even if I really think she was actually a spy.

We're through the window and listening for signs of life, or another person in the house apart from Red. We're also listening to the man at the door trying to get rid of a Polish builder.

This room looks familiar. It looks very like the the room we broke into the time we raided his old house, with a similar computer and a similar booby trapped filing cabinet which we totally leave alone. While I mind getting captured, I mind even more about being blown up and would much rather just grab Red and get out of here.

I can see that Keira wants to play with the computer so signal that I'll search the other rooms. This also means that if I get into trouble I've got Keira to try and rescue me rather than the other way around which wouldn't be much use.

Guess who I've just found?

Well, it's not a difficult question is it.

Red is handcuffed to a bed and has been gagged. I take a quick photo, to tease her about later, but then notice that she's crying.

Whispering, I ask if she's hurt and she shakes her head. At the same time I'm attacking the lock on the handcuffs with one of my lock picks which is a handy little tool for opening such things. It's also probably illegal to be carrying these around but I'm in so much trouble already if we get caught that a drop more isn't going to make any difference.

While I've been telling you all this I've managed to spring the lock and open the cuff releasing Red's hand. A few moments later and we're quietly heading back to the office and out of the window, collecting Keira on the way. She's attached some string to one of the filing cabinet drawers and feeds it out of the window as we leave. Once me and Red are over the fence, she gives the string a sharp tug and then wishes she hadn't.

First, there's the sound of a small explosion followed by a wailing alarm loud enough to be heard from right by the park entrance which is where we're now trying to look like a family out for a stroll. I've never seen Keira get over a fence that quickly before.

Time to disappear I think.

On the way back to the flat Keira questions Red and makes sure it's still safe to go back there and that boss man doesn't know where we're living. Unfortunately I think he can guess who rescued Red which sort of gives him a clue that we're still all together and so must be somewhere close by. But how did he find Red in the first place?

While this is going on I phone Jack and tell him we've succeeded and it's ok to come home.

"I thought something must have happened with the bang and all. We're both safe and on our way."

Apparently Jack had babbled something about being illegal immigrant and "not wanting police find him" as he ran away down the street. But by then, our enemy was already rushing upstairs to find out what was going on.

Back at the flat Keira insists we put our grab bags within easy reach before we debrief. In case you don't know, a grab bag is filled with essential items like a change of underwear and anything else you might need if you have to run away from somewhere quickly and leave everything else behind.

It's one of Keira's little rituals to check our bags regularly and make sure we don't just spread things around the flat.

"You can't afford 5 minutes to find your lock picks Jamie if it's an emergency."

She even woke us up one night and timed how quickly we could get to her car. Oh, and she forgot to mention that it was only a practise run which is why I then needed to quickly find a bush to pee behind.

Which reminds me of what else I need to do before we debrief.

Prison

I knew it would happen eventually.

I'm in prison.

Actually, we're all in prison and there's nothing we can do about it until we come up with a plan of escape.

What we should have done is grab our bags and run but instead Keira has locked us in the flat and told everyone that we have some highly catchable disease and have got to stay away from people for a week.

Jack is the only one allowed in and that's only because he brings us food.

Red has also told us her story which answers some of the questions I had.

"I was just on my way to the film when he came up and stopped me."

So she didn't just dump me with Dog Girl then. I think I owe her a silent apology.

"He said that he'd already found Jamie and that if I wanted to see him alive again then I was to follow him and not make a fuss."

What a liar!

Him, not her I mean.

"Then when we got to the house he took my bag and locked me in the bedroom saying I could see Jamie later."

Well, that bit proved true although probably not quite how he expected it.

"He was dead chuffed..."

She means very happy.

"...and I could hear him on the phone."

Seems he'd forgotten that there was another phone in the bedroom and all Red had to do was pick it up to listen in to the conversation. Sometimes evil enemy agents can be just as dumb as the rest of us.

Either boss man has another job as well or else he was talking in code because he told this chap that he'd got one of the books that this man had been looking for and hoped to get the others soon. It wasn't damaged at the moment but he hadn't examined it in detail yet.

I think this means that he's found one of us and will get the rest once he's questioned Red. Good job we got there first!

"I reckon this book buyer was boss man's boss because he got told off for phoning him at work."

Who told who off? Red can get confusing at times but I suppose being kidnapped and then suddenly rescued can scramble your brain a bit.

Apparently the book buyer was very upset about being phoned at work. I wonder why?

Can't be much of a job being an enemy agent if you have to have a proper job as well. Perhaps it's cover and he's only pretending to be a milkman or a book seller or whatever he is. Maybe when I grow up I'll have to pretend to be something as well as being a secret ninja.

I wonder what it will be?

I'm not very good at reading so it will have to be something which doesn't involve books. Or perhaps I can have a computer that will translate for me; that would be cool.

I miss the next bit of the conversation as I'm worrying about my new job. My old teacher used to recognise when I did this sort of thing and would come over and whisper in my ear.

"Mission Control to Jamie! Time to come back to Earth, Jamie."

She was nice like that and made sure I tried to concentrate on what she was saying unlike now when I've obviously missed something important because the girls have started crying.

"Yes, I know it's sad but what else can we do?" Keira says.

"Our cover's blown and people will be looking for us, asking questions. Don't forget, they've got our pictures as well. We can't stay in this flat forever and we can't go to school either. Soon someone is going to recognise us and then we'll all be in big trouble. We've no choice but to run."

It's true. It doesn't make it any easier but it's still true. We have to run. But where? We've got no Plan B and no secret bolt hole. We've no passports and no friends with big country mansions or hidden lairs on hard to get to islands.

"Phone Dad," I blurt out.

Don't know where that came from but Keira thinks it's a sensible idea if we do it properly. I know that she's friendly with Dad and that he'd sent her to keep an eye on me when he moved out.

I also know that Keira is very careful which is why Jack is now being taught his lines.

"Don't use your own phone and destroy the one you do use, or use a public telephone. No, don't do that in case they can get access to the street cameras. Get a mobile from somewhere."

Keira is being very cautious.

"Phone this number and ask for Mr Gladstone, Mr Simon Gladstone, say exactly that and no more. He'll tell you that you've got the wrong number so just hang up."

Jack looks confused.

"Then what?" he asks.

"Then nothing. Ditch the phone and make sure you're not being followed. Then just do normal stuff but stay away from here for a couple of days. We've got enough food to last until then."

She then explains that "Mr Gladstone, Mr Simon Gladstone" is code.

Dad will know that Keira needs to speak to him and, like Jack, will go find a new mobile to make the call.

All we can do now is wait and hope that the enemy aren't too quick at finding us.

"Aardvark?"

"Anteater?"

"Purple spotted sea monkey?"

Red wins. She's played this game with me before and knows about purple spotted sea monkeys and three humped penguins and all of the other pretend animals I make up to cheat in this game.

Yes, we're that bored that we're playing 'Guess the Animal'.

'I Spy' gets even more boring, even more quickly when you've only got one room to play in and we've lost the pack of cards somewhere so can't play 'Snap'.

I'm about to get into an argument with Naz about using pretend animals when Keira's phone rings.

"Yes?"

She's being careful.

"Tell me something I don't know."

Now I don't know what she's being.

She switches the phone to speaker mode so we can all hear Dad's voice.

"Yellow, Green, Red. Never mixed."

It's definitely Dad. Not many people know about my socks and the order I wear them in during the week.

Keira is still being careful and keeps the call short so that it can't be easily traced.

I don't understand all of the words but after the call she explains.

"No, I've only got three kittens left but they need to go to a good home and I don't really want to separate them." isn't really about kittens and,

"No, I think the mum's got to go as well, the vet wants to put her down."

That's telling him that Keira has got to relocate as well because someone wants to kill her.

She didn't actually tell us that bit; I figured it out for myself. I mean, why go to all the bother of keep searching for us otherwise?

They want us dead!

Drill

Why would anyone want me dead?

Ok, I know I can be annoying at times, or so Red has told me, but I'm never that annoying.

And why would they want to kill Red, and Naz, and Keira as well?

It doesn't make sense.

I've been here before. Not being under threat of death, not real death, but I've been confused before; lots of times actually.

Miss S, my old teacher had a cure though.

"If it doesn't make sense Jamie, then you're missing something. Have you read the question properly? Have you missed some important information?"

Usually it's because I haven't read the question properly; I'm good at that.

But I'm not reading now and I'm still confused.

Why spend all this time and effort searching for us? Why are we so important?

"Jamie, you've gone very quiet, what's the matter?"

Red's come into my room to find me. I explain my problem but leave out the killing bit as I don't want her crying again.

Seems I've had a good idea, which is why we're now all sitting around the table over supper and all trying to answer this one question.

Why are we so important?

We know what boss man looks like but so what? Dad already knew that when we first started following him so it can't be that.

What else do we know?

"He's responsible for the bombs 'cos we saw the map on his computer when we broke into his old house."

"He used to go to my church."

"He smells."

Red's been closer to him that the rest of us.

We don't know very much do we.

The conversation sort of stops there and we all decide that it's time for bed which is why I'm now counting sheep again. It's what I do when I can't get to sleep.

The sheep turn into kittens and someone is throwing books at them and the ground is shaking. It must be an earthquake and I've got to go and hide under a table but I can't move as someone has now grabbed my arms.

“Jamie, wake up!”

Why is Keira whispering?

“Emergency exit!”

Not another drill! Haven’t we had enough excitement for one day? I know she’s worried about us but we know how to do this and don’t need another practice, especially tonight.

“Jamie, now!”

I bundle into last night’s clothes still piled at the bottom of my bed. I’m probably wearing the wrong socks but it’s not really morning yet so it’s not totally wrong.

Still half asleep, I stagger into the kitchen with my grab bag to see Keira stuffing food into another empty bag.

“Go help the girls and get everything into the car, now!”

Keira really likes her pretend emergencies.

Why is she starting the car? She's never done that before. She's supposed to check her watch and tell us how slow we've been and then we all go back to bed. Why am I not going back to bed?

"Jamie, it's not a drill. Now shut up and listen while I drive."

Keira's just had a call from Dad who's just had a call from a friend who's just been told to get to our town immediately with a snatch squad. Somehow we're now being hunted by the good guys as well as the bad guys because Dad's friend is a spy and he's definitely on the right side.

What's going on?

I can understand the bad guys wanting to kill us. Actually I can't, but ignore that for the moment. What I don't understand is why do the good guys want us as well?

Anyway, as soon as Keira got the call she got us moving and here we are except that I don't know where here is and I don't know where we're going. At least I have company. None of us know where we're going, including Keira who's doing the driving.

I think we're in trouble.

The girls are told to lie down in the back of the car so that it looks like there's just the two of us. Hopefully they'll be looking for four people and not two.

Keira throws her phone at me and I have to call Jack and then switch the speaker on so she can talk and drive at the same time.

"Jack honey, it's me."

He'll know somethings up; she never calls anyone Honey!

"The car's packed in. Can you come get me?"

Of course he can.

"Yeah, I'm at Sharon's."

Apparently this pretend Sharon lives in a nearby village which is where Jack meets us twenty minutes later.

If the good guys are after us then they'll have all the benefits of our country's anti-terrorist systems which means we need to change cars.

Hold on a minute! Now I'm a terrorist?

Apparently they can find out the registration of Keira's car at the click of a few computer keys and then get all of the traffic cameras to look for it. That's why Jack will be driving it in the opposite direction and on the nearby motorway which has lots of cameras. Hopefully, this will make them chase him rather than us.

Keira then uses Jack's phone to call Dad and arrange for some new wheels to be delivered to our old mate by the river. More code which means that Dad will now have another car ready for us when we get to wherever they've jut agreed to meet.

This is logical. If Jack gets caught driving Keira's car then they'll start looking for his car as well. If I didn't know better, I'd think that Keira's had training in evading capture which makes me think that she's definitely a spy or has been at some time.

Keira reckons that we'll have an hour or so before Jack gets caught which will give us just about enough time to get to Dad.

We have a plan!

It's not much of a plan but at least we now have somewhere to go and something to go in that won't get us captured for at least an hour.

Did I mention that life as a Red Sock Ninja can get a bit too exciting at times?

Poo

Have you ever seen any film where the hero has to stop for a poo?

No, I haven't either which is why Keira is showing me what to do behind this tree.

I've never been so embarrassed in my life!

At least she disappears before I take my trousers down and lean back against this tree. She also makes sure I've got a roll of toilet paper handy. I'll spare you the rest of the details but I'll never take an indoor toilet for granted ever again.

Back on the road Keira explains that in the wild you'd dig a small hole to poo in and use leaves to wipe your bottom. Yuk!

Then you could spray some pepper over it before you bury everything to stop the smell being picked up by tracker dogs. What I just left behind could be picked up by short nosed Australian moles with a heavy cold. As I said before, Yuk! At least the girls find it funny judging from the giggling coming from the back seat.

"Perhaps you can be our new secret weapon Jamie."

Thanks Red.

Keira's had a good look at the map while we were stopped and now drives right to the meeting spot where Dad is already parked, waiting for us. As we change cars, careful to take absolutely everything with us, including sweet wrappers, Dad tells me to jump in the back seat with the girls. He's coming with us.

While we've been busy escaping Dad has come up with a plan of sorts.

"We need all of you to disappear, leaving a nice trail behind you which will keep everybody busy for a few days. While they're chasing after fairy dust, we can get you hidden properly."

We stop near a big railway station somewhere and park well away from any cameras. Keira then borrows Dad's coat and, wearing a pair of dark glasses, disappears into the booking office. Dad explains that she's going to book us tickets to the ferry terminal and then will use a nearby phone to reserve tickets on a boat to Ireland.

I'm not sure I want to go on a boat but Naz says they're cool. You can watch the seagulls and go and have burger and chips and even go to sleep if you want to.

Sleep sounds a good idea and I start yawning.

The sound of the door slamming shut and the engine starting wakes me up. Why are we driving? I thought we were going on a train to the boat.

“Jamie, stop being thick.”

Thanks Keira, like I’ve done this sort of thing lots of times before. I don’t know what’s going on.

“That’s where we want them to think we’re going.”

Ah, now I see.

Dad joins in.

“While they’re looking for us there, we’re all going on a different holiday. Somewhere nice and quiet with not many visitors.”

When we eventually get there, I can see why nobody wants to visit.

It's a dump. A derelict. A disaster.

I get told to shut up by three different female voices at once. Guess I'm outvoted.

Inside isn't much better but I keep this to myself and let the girls decide for themselves while Dad puts the kettle on. At least we've got electricity and running water and hopefully I won't need to go find a tree every time I need a poo.

What happens if you can't find a tree? What about if you're stuck in the middle of a desert? I suppose you'd have to lean up against a friendly camel and hope she didn't wander off while you're…

"Jamie, are you listening?"

"Yes Miss," I say automatically before realising where I am.

When the laughing stops, Dad reminds me that I don't have to call him Miss and that we're still trying to work out why we're so important.

"It must have something to do with the first time we found that nasty man from church," Naz suggests.

She's right. It all started then.

So, what are we missing?

Well, we're missing Keira for a start. She's disappeared to the bathroom and has been gone ages. I hope she opens the window afterwards.

Keira comes back and I've suddenly decided to stop drinking my hot chocolate. The water is poisonous. It must be, because look what it's done to Keira's hair!

I'd just got used to her being blond and now the water has turned her hair green. I start to panic. I don't want green hair or green anything.

Why do people keep laughing at me and why is Keira holding up that small bottle?

“Hair dye, Jamie. I’ve dyed my hair.”

Oh.

If we’re to stay here then someone has got to go shopping and so Keira needs to change her appearance.

After three days stuck indoors, we all want to go shopping but it’s not going to happen.

“Sorry guys, but you’re all just too difficult to disguise. If anyone does start searching up here, then three new kids will stand out enough as it is without them even knowing what you look like.”

As a special treat, we do go out together the following night but it isn’t to the pictures or anything. No, instead I’m kneeling by this tree and trying to look invisible hoping that one of the others will walk past so that I can ambush them.

The Red Sock Ninja Clan are on a night exercise.

Dad has got Red and Naz, and I'm with Keira and, except for Dad, we're all in full ninja gear. He's shown us how to paint our faces so that we blend in with the trees and stuff and now we're finding our way around and trying to avoid the other group.

"This is a recon patrol. Your task is to produce a map of the area with three hiding places and two lookout points."

It's just like playing soldiers.

Not that I play with soldiers now that I'm a big boy. I mean, if I was at home I'd be changing schools next term and I'm sure that they don't play with toys at big school and besides, mine are still under my bed back at our flat.

What was that?

Something just sort of shrieked!

"Owl," whispers Keira.

Can owls attack you? There's so much I don't know about the

countryside. Do you get cows in the forest? What about sheep, do they bite?

A tap on the shoulder tells me it's time to move.

Snakes!

What about snakes?

Peter Marney

Lessons

I have not been savaged by a sheep or stung by a snake or crushed by a cow. I did manage to find a nettle bush but Keira's just put some white stuff on the rash and it doesn't itch any more.

Now I can look at the map the girls have drawn and add in the bits I found.

It's not much of a map and Dad decides that we all need to go back to school which is sort of why we're now playing with radios.

They're not proper radios which can play music and stuff but the old type which were sort of like mobiles before we had mobiles. Not that we have mobiles any more. They're all sitting in our grab bags in pieces.

"Take out the battery and remove the card."

Red shows me what to do.

"Even when it's off, a mobile can be traced, so no mobiles."

Instead we now have these boxy things with aerials sticking out of the top. We also have to learn new codes.

"Two buzzes means are you there and one buzz?"

It's question time but we don't have to put our hands up.

"One buzz means I'm listening," says Naz. She's quick at picking up codes and stuff.

There's short buzzes and long buzzes and combinations of both and they all mean something different.

The most important one is three short buzzes which means danger approaching and it's the one I'm frantically now signalling to Red and Naz.

We're back in our playground, it's the middle of the night, and we're being attacked.

I've just seen an enemy soldier making his way towards our farmhouse and I'm warning the girls.

It's about now that someone clamps a hand over my face and whispers in my ear while I nearly wet myself.

"Bang, bang. You're dead soldier boy!"

I hate Keira.

I hate the way she sneaks up on you in the night and the way she kills you before you've got a chance to run away or anything.

She doesn't make it any better back at the house.

"I wouldn't have really shot you Jamie."

Thanks.

"No, best to use a knife. Slit your throat nice and quietly."

Did I mention I hate this game?

The girls fell for the same trick as well which is why we're now working as a team, proper ninja style. That way, the enemy can't sneak up on us.

We've also now made proper lookout and hiding places. We've got three escape routes and two different meeting spots. If they do find us then we've now got a chance of escape.

I've also learned how to hide and when to stay hidden.

"Just 'cos I've walked past you doesn't mean that I won't double back for another look and doesn't mean that I've not got a friend some way behind me just to catch you if you try to follow."

Still and silent. Ears and eyes open and mouth half shut. Communicate by buzzes and use the earpieces not the speakers.

I don't have to count sheep anymore. I'm so tired after our outdoor lessons that I fall asleep before I've even got into my pyjamas.

That got me into more trouble.

"I know you like routine Jamie but you're going to have to learn some new habits."

What do you do when you go to bed?

Brush your teeth, jimjams, a bit of your book and then lights out?

No, you're doing it all wrong.

Grab bag here, shoes here, clothes there. Check all exits clear and keys in the locks. Then teeth, book and bed. No jimjams. Either nothing at all or pants and tee shirt.

"It's all about time Jamie," explains Dad.

"Seconds count in an emergency. Having to get out of pyjamas and into clothes can cost you time and get you captured. So, new routine!"

The girls go through the same changes and we're back to Keira's little emergencies in the middle of the day or night. We got our own back though and called an emergency in the middle of her shower one morning. That was funny.

The next day, Keira gets her revenge by turning one of the bedrooms into a gym. That's why I'm now pushing my nose away from the floor for the twentieth time and why the girls are fighting each other.

"You've all been slacking and it's time you got fit again. We can't go running so this is then next best thing."

No it isn't.

Doing press ups and pretend boxing is nothing like a nice long jog but I know what is.

Keira takes a lot of persuading but eventually allows me to go get my music. She takes even more persuading to join in but has to give up when the girls won't stop nagging her. That's why I'm now being told off for laughing.

It also helps if you can imagine Keira in a pink fluffy tutu.

In case you don't know, a tutu is what girls wear for ballet and we've just convinced Keira to go through one of our morning warm up routines from school. I'm just sad that we don't have a full length mirror so that I can compare my usual inelegant moves to the mess Keira is making. I've never really got the hang of ballet but Naz has trained for years and Red, although new to it, has picked it up quite well. I think the street dancing helped her as she's used to learning moves and remembering sequences.

Delightfully, Keira is just as hopeless as me but at the end of half an hour agrees that it's just as good a workout as a run.

We take turns in the shower afterwards and then settle down to some breakfast and fresh rolls which Dad has collected from the village.

"Looks like we've got some very nosy neighbours," he reports.

"Every shop I went into I got the third degree."

I remember degrees from my maths lessons but not the third degree, or even the first or second ones. Dad thinks it comes from old detective stories and means asking people lots of questions which is exactly what's been happening to him this morning.

"Nothing too obvious, but just a bit more than the usual good morning and how are you sort of thing."

Why can't people just say what they mean and stop talking about degrees and stuff? No wonder I have trouble understanding what's going on when even my own Dad speaks in code.

I guess that the village people like to chat as there's not much else to do around here. It's not like there's a big shopping centre or cinema or library or skate park or anything really apart from a few shops and a church.

"I suppose they're just trying to be friendly," he says, "that's why they've invited us to church."

Peter Marney

Church

No, I'm not in church.

I'm stuck up a tree and have my face painted like a soldier.

Somewhere else in the woods you'll find Red and Naz doing the same thing but you'll have to search really carefully as we've gotten very good at hiding.

While Dad and Keira are singing hymns somewhere, we've been packed out of the house and into the woods just in case.

"In case of what?" I asked.

I didn't realise but my Dad can be just as suspicious as Keira.

"In case someone decides to take a look at the house while the mysterious new strangers are safe in church."

Well, I must admit, it does sound like a good idea especially if you've got nothing else to gossip about. I can hear them now.

"I took a stroll up to the old farmhouse last Sunday and guess what I found?"

Not much if we've done our work properly.

If anyone breaks into the house today, all they're going to find is the evidence of the nice couple who are down at the church and making new friends. No kids, no ninjas, and nothing at all suspicious.

All of our clothes and stuff have been bundled into bundles and stashed in secret places away from prying eyes. Our own prying eyes are meanwhile on the lookout for anyone who just happens to come calling.

Or walking her dog.

Did I mention that I hate dogs?

We've never got on and I think it's something to do with the curse of Jamie.

Every animal that I've ever owned has either died or disappeared. That's why I never got too close to the school fish, or any other pet I come across, including and most especially dogs.

To me, a dog is a walking poo machine with a tail at one end and a nose at the other. A nose which is very good at smelling; which is just what we don't want at the moment.

As I said before, we've got very good at hiding from humans but dogs are another thing entirely. Put very simply, Red smells.

She's not the only one. Naz smells as well and so do I. In fact everyone smells. We all smell and dogs are very good at picking up smells both animal and human. That's why the police have special dogs which can smell out things.

I don't think this one's a police dog though as its owner doesn't look anything like a policewoman, although she could be in heavy disguise and just pretending to be some old lady who likes poking her nose into other people's business.

She's just knocked on our door and is now going around the house and looking in all of the windows. Her dog is snuffling about as well but luckily she has it on a lead.

Had it on a lead.

The stupid woman has just decided to unleash the smelly monster so that it can go and pee against one of our trees and generally make a nuisance of itself.

"Go on Max, good boy! See what you can find."

Suspicious witch.

What does she think he's going to find? Three secret ninjas hiding in the bushes?

I hope not.

Max seems to like our trees judging by the way his tail is wagging and he's dashing about all over the place. Then, of course, he decides to come in my direction. Anyone would think I have an inbuilt dog magnet or something.

He starts snuffling about under my tree and then begins to bark.

"Good boy Max, what you found then?"

It's a stupid name for a dog and it looks like I might just get the opportunity to tell her in person.

"Rabbits? Is it rabbits boy?"

Since when do rabbits climb trees?

Fortunately that idea hasn't struck her yet and she's content to search through the bushes with her stick. Another couple of paces and I'll be able to pee right on top of her head. Of course, if she looks up she's also got a good chance of staring straight into my eyes.

"Can I help you?"

Have I told you that Keira is my most favourite person in the whole wide world? I'll even forgive her blasting away on her high pitched whistle which has made Max turn and gallop towards her.

"What a lovely dog."

That's a matter of opinion!

"I'd hate him to get hurt."

She's bending over and stroking Max while talking to his owner.

"You won't believe the problem we've been having with rabbits.

That's why we've set the traps. Nasty things but Simon says it's all we can do until he brings his shotguns down."

Who's Simon and what's all this about traps? Nobody mentioned that there's traps in the woods! Nobody mentioned guns either.

"I'd hate to see a lovely dog like this caught in a snare chasing after rabbits. I'm Samantha by the way, how are you?"

Keira's holding the dog by its collar in one hand and has the other stretched out towards the lady owner.

"Best put him back on the lead if I were you. Sorry I can't offer you a cup of tea but I've just popped back to put the oven on. Completely forgot in the rush. If you want to hang on a second, I'll walk back to church with you."

As if Keira's going to give her the choice!

"Such a lovely area, not that we've seen much of it yet of course but we'll have to start looking soon. That's if the relocation goes through. All a bit hush-hush at the moment but Simon thought we'd better come down and see for ourselves. It's that or Dubai and I can't see myself wearing one of those hijab things can you?"

Samantha's a right little chatterbox. I don't think I've ever heard Keira prattle on like this before or give so much information away.

Shame it's all a pack of lies.

Rabbits

After church, Dad and Keira scout around to make sure that we don't have any more unwanted visitors before allowing us down from the trees and back into the house. It's all done very quietly and quickly and before long I'm in the shower again and trying to get rid of my Green Man disguise.

Over lunch, they tell us about church and I update them on the antics of the nosy woman. We decide not to get too worried about her visit as she's clearly not one of the enemy.

The rest of the villagers were equally keen to get information and now know about the traps and the shotguns and also that Dad isn't really a patient hunter.

"Can't stand all this skulking about waiting for the game to show itself so I just blast away at the bushes if I hear anything."

That should keep the woods free of accidental picnickers or villagers who just happen to lose their way and find our house.

A temporary victory but over the wrong enemy. Boss man and his gang are still looking for us. So are the good guys which is still something I don't understand.

"Did your mate ask why they had to snatch us Dad?" I ask.

"No, it doesn't work like that Jamie. You just do what you're told and then forget about it."

Sounds a bit like school, except for the forgetting part. Miss likes us to remember what she tells us.

That gives me an idea.

"Let's play a game."

Everyone sighs.

"No, let's play a game where we tell the story of our raids on the enemy. Then Red can tell us about her capture again."

They still don't seem too interested.

"If we all tell the story together then perhaps we'll remember more of it. There's got to be a clue somewhere about why we're still being chased."

And that's how we spend the afternoon; arguing about whether I wore blue jeans or my black trousers and whether Dad went through the window first or Red did.

It's amazing how everyone sees the same thing differently. Dad says it's like cars.

"As soon as you buy a different car, suddenly the road is full of other people with the same model."

It isn't really. He explains that because you've now got a super VJ900 or whatever, your brain is now programmed to spot all of the other VJ900s that you previously ignored.

So maybe my idea isn't such a bad one after all. If we all see things a bit differently then between us we should be able to build up a much bigger and better picture of what really went on.

It's six o'clock by the time we finish storytelling but we still haven't found the vital clue which will explain everything. Guess life isn't like the detective stories you read about in comics or watch on the television.

The great thing about Sunday nights at the moment is that we don't have any homework to finish for Monday morning. We don't have any school to get ready for either; well, not any normal school. Keira is still teaching us tradecraft as she calls it, which seems to be all about being a spy in the countryside.

Do you know what rabbit tastes like?

I didn't but I do now. I also know how to catch one and it's not nice. It involves tying a thin wire loop to a stake in the ground somewhere where the rabbit might run. If it does, then the loop tightens around it's leg or neck and the poor thing is trapped. Dad shows us how to set the traps and later how to kill Mr Bunny.

"No, it's not nice, but if you're out in the wild then you can't just pop down to the shops for food. If you can't catch food then you will starve and a starving ninja is no good to anyone."

If killing the rabbit wasn't bad enough, Keira shows us how to prepare it for cooking. Trust me, you don't want to know!

It does taste good though even if it's now keeping me awake.

I spend the time going over the story we put together.

"If it doesn't make sense Jamie, then you're missing something. Have you read the question properly? Have you missed some important information?"

Can I have a clue please Miss?

She's not being helpful and hops away with her big floppy ears twitching in the sunlight. It must be time for the register because I can hear a man's voice calling out names.

“Thomas, Thompson, Travis, Valcheck, Wall, Wallace."

I’m waiting for my name to be called but I can’t answer because my neck’s caught in a wire noose and someone’s shaking me.

“Jamie, wake up!”

Why is Red waking me up in the middle of the night and why is everyone else looking through the doorway?

Over a cup of hot chocolate they tell me about the scream.

I don’t remember screaming but apparently I did, and woke up the whole house. I sort of half remember a giant rabbit and then something important which I’ve now forgotten again.

Naz starts yawning which sets everyone else off.

Have you ever played that game on the bus where you pretend to yawn? Do it a couple of times and soon everyone else is joining in. I bet you're even yawning yourself now as you read this.

Anyway, yawning is catching and everyone but me now wants to go back to bed.

Red decides that she'll come and chat to me until I drift off to sleep again which is why she's now sharing my pillow as we stare at the ceiling and try to make a map of the discoloured paint.

That gets boring very quickly so I get her to tell me again what happened when she got captured. Maybe this time she'll remember something different.

I'm sort of half drifting off to sleep again as I listen to Red's voice when something jerks me awake again.

"Say it again!"

Red doesn't understand.

"You said he was on the phone to the other man. What exactly happened?"

She goes through the details again.

"I picked up the phone in the bedroom and it was quiet. Then a female voice said that Mr Williamson was busy and our man got all angry and shouted that it was of the utmost urgency. Then he got put through."

The utmost urgency.

Guess we're really important.

I wonder why?

Peter Marney

Names

Do you like jigsaw puzzles?

I'm usually very good at solving them because I can hold the picture on the box in my mind and sort of see where the bits go.

That's why I'm annoyed with myself at the moment. Our problem is like a big jigsaw puzzle and I'm missing a piece. The trouble is, I think it's hiding right in front of me but I just can't see it. I think it might be half hidden under another bit of the puzzle but where?

Keira's found a way to stop me dreaming but I'm not too keen on it.

She's decided that if I'm totally exhausted by the time I go to bed I'll be too tired to dream and will just go right off to sleep. That's why I'm getting to do most of the chores in the house and have a double helping of workouts each day. It's also why I'm starting to sort of drift off even if I'm standing up and in the middle of something.

"Jamie? Jamie! Wake up! I've been calling your name for ages."

Now what does she want?

I don't actually listen to anything for the next few minutes and just sit there smiling.

I've found the piece, or at least I think I can see a corner of it peeking out.

"Jamie, will you please stop smiling while I'm telling you off. What's so funny?"

It's been sitting there all this time and we just couldn't see it. Or maybe it was that chat to Red which dislodged the missing bit of information.

I manage to get out of the telling off by shouting "Eureka!" and then by running around in circles getting everyone sitting around the table.

"Eureka!" means "I've got it" in Greek and has something to do with some important old Greek man, a crown, and a bath. Oh, and he run around without any clothes on as well, which is something I am definitely not doing at the moment.

"It's names! It's all about the names!"

Dad had been looking through a long list of names when we suddenly had to rush out of the enemies hideout.

"You remember Dad. You saw all those names all the way up to W before we had to escape quickly."

That's why we're so important. Not for what we found but for what we didn't find.

"That's why we couldn't figure it out. They're still after us because they think we saw a very important name, one which Dad didn't get down to."

Dad starts to ask a question but I've still got one of my own to ask.

"Red, what was the name of the man who couldn't be interrupted?"

That's the clue.

"Mr Williamson?"

Dad stops trying to interrupt to ask his question. He just sits there stunned.

"What's so important about the name?"

Even Red hasn't made the connection.

Dad's boss, who is supposed to be one of the good guys, is called Mr Williamson. Now maybe it's a coincidence but you've got to ask why boss man, a proven enemy would be calling up someone with the same name as one of our spy chiefs to tell him about us.

I can see Keira working it all out in her head.

"It makes sense. They think we've spotted the connection but don't realise it ourselves. So the easiest thing is to find us and make sure we don't tell anyone else."

We're back to being killed again.

"But it's still not proof Jamie. There's nothing to link them apart from a name on a list which we didn't actually see. You can't hang a man without proof."

Do they still hang people? I thought we'd stopped that ages ago.

Maybe they still hang traitors; because a spy chief who also secretly works for the other side is definitely a traitor as far as I'm concerned.

Well, at least we now think we know what they think we know, which is why we're so important in their eyes. Now we just need to find some proof apart from the word of a girl with red hair.

"Naz, can you do another drawing of your friend from church?"

I've got an idea. Naz is really, really good at drawing and her best drawings look just like a photograph.

Now all we need is to get this new drawing to Mr Williamson without being caught.

When we were still a family, Mum would have this thing at Christmas time of guessing who'd sent the Christmas card before she opened it. I used to think she had magical powers until she explained the trick to me.

"I look at the writing on the envelope Jamie."

Everybody's got different handwriting. Mine's a bit of a scrawl but Naz has beautiful writing just like a teacher. Mum could recognise the writing of whoever had sent the card. But, and this is the important part, the trick wasn't so good once people started using computer printed labels for their envelopes.

There's another reason that trick would be difficult these days. People don't write very much now that we have computers and hardly anyone sends letters anymore. Yes, I know we have to write in school and even the teacher writes in our books but in real life, how many people do you see writing?

While Naz is busy drawing, I explain the rest of my plan to the others.

“It’s an idea Jamie, and it’s got a slim chance of working but where does it get us? Boss man and all the others will just disappear for a while and come back stronger.”

I hadn’t thought of that.

I rather hoped that we could sort everything out and go home, or if not home, at least back to our flat and school. I never thought I’d say it but I miss school. Not the proper lessons; most of the teachers are rubbish. I miss all the other stuff like dancing and doing shows and generally messing about with our mates. I even miss Dog Girl a little bit.

I do think it’s about time that Red and Naz went home though. I know they miss their Mums and I expect their families miss them as well.

I need a better plan.

Despatches

I've decided what I want to be when I grow up.

I used to think that I wanted to be a train driver or a fireman but that's what all little boys want. I'm not a little boy any more and I want to be a despatch rider.

They get to wear cool leather suits and ride these big powerful motorbikes. I'm not sure about the bright "hi-vis" jackets though, they sort of spoil the super hero look.

"Nah, you need one of those the way them idiots drive these days," grins Zak. "Nobody looks out for bikes on the road until they run you over."

He's one of Keira's many friends and he's lending us his bike and gear. The bike itself is really cool and completely matt black with a huge engine which just purrs like a cat rather than roaring like a lion.

He seems pretty relaxed about Keira riding his bike and I hope she doesn't crash it as this would sort of ruin the plan.

Have you ever watched a spider hunting?

It sits there in the middle of its web just waiting for lunch to come blundering into its trap. Each of its legs is carefully balanced on each strand of the web and it can tell as soon as anything disturbs the spider silk.

That's the problem with Mr Williamson. He's sitting in the middle of a city, in the middle of his spy web, and there's no way we can get to him without twitching one of the strands of spider silk. So the problem became how to trap the spider without turning into lunch ourselves and the answer is easy. You wait for the spider to leave the web.

It seems that our spider likes to spend the week at work in the city but goes home at the weekends to his place in the country.

"We all went there once," said Dad. "It was a big celebration for something or another and the whole department got invited down for the day for tea and games on the lawn."

Sounds like one of my birthday parties, back when I used to have such things and before Dad left.

"Anyway, it's a big place in the country with its own grounds."

Dad explains that the house has its own sort of private park with a big wall around the outside and alarms, lots of alarms.

"Not the sort of place you'd want to try and break into Jamie, not even with the Red Sock Ninjas."

Which is why Keira is walking up to the front door.

I'd love to describe to you what happens next but all we've got is what's coming out of our two way radio. Keira's got hers strapped to her hi vis jacket and, although it doesn't look like it, it's broadcasting to us back in the car.

"Hand delivery, Mr Williams?" she says.

We hear a voice correct her.

"Mr Williamson perhaps? That's me. It's a bit late isn't it?"

We've timed it so that it's just getting dark.

"Says urgent on the job sheet, so urgent it is Guv."

The handset crackles.

"Where do I sign?"

Just before we hear the door closing we hear Keira again.

"Dispatch from Red One. Job complete. Got anything else for me Norman?"

I think Keira likes being a despatch rider.

It's as easy as that and all we can do now is wait.

It doesn't take long.

Soon we watch as a small car hurries out of the gates and heads towards the main road and then the motorway.

You'd think that it's easy to follow someone at night but it isn't, especially when you're the only other car on the road. That's why we don't try.

We leave that job to Keira who has now removed her "Hi-viz" jacket and is all dressed in black leather. She's also riding without lights and completely disappears in the dark.

Yes, I know it's really dangerous to ride without lights but Keira doesn't want to be seen and especially not by someone who'll be looking out for followers. The man's a spy after all.

Plus she's not really in the dark. We've equipped the bike with this special light which you can only see by wearing special goggles just like the ones over Keira's helmet. So to her it's like she's riding in daylight.

We listen to Keira giving us directions and trail after at a safe distance. When we get to the motorway, we take over as the lead vehicle and follow Mr Williamson all the way north until he turns off towards another town. For some reason he appears to be in a hurry.

I'm beginning to see a pattern here.

Our spider leads us all the way into town and then down some streets where he parks outside a normal looking house. We carry on straight past with me and the girls ducking down in case he happens to glance at our car. Keira's already stopped short of the house and has fished out her small pair of binoculars.

"Guess who's answered the door?" she asks over the two way radio.

It seems that our spider has taken us right to the door of boss man. Now how did he know where to find him I wonder?

Dad then makes another phone call and a few minutes later things get very exciting.

It starts off with a couple of police cars blocking off the road. Then another couple of vans arrive and we can see that some of these new policemen have guns. That's when we get a tap on the window.

"Sorry sir but we're going to have to ask you to move the car please."

Dad innocently asks what's happening.

"Nothing to get worried about sir. Just best to get the kids out of the way. Quick as you can please."

He looks worried and is definitely lying but we drive off anyway.

We do get a running commentary from Keira though who's managed to hide herself in sight of the house.

"Here comes the heavy mob," she whispers.

Then we hear the crash of a door being smashed open and then lots of shouting.

"Armed police! Get down on the floor and hands on heads! Armed Police!"

You get the idea.

Then it all goes very quiet until two men get taken away in a police van. I wonder who they might be?

Peter Marney

Secrets

You'd expect such a thing to make the news programmes but guess what?

Not a whisper.

It's as if the raid and capture of a major criminal had never happened.

So much for the Red Sock Ninjas careful plans. Well, if they're going to keep secrets then so are we!

Keira takes the girls back to school until things settle down and

I get to go live with Dad for a while. I also get to speak to some serious looking people about what happened when I got kidnapped and what I overheard on the phone.

I know that's not how it actually happened but I don't want to get the Red Sock Ninjas into trouble and it makes more sense for boss man to have recognised me as I'm the son of one of his targets. Plus it's got to be true because we've got a selfie of me on my phone handcuffed to his bed. It's date stamped and everything!

Did I mention how good some of Keira's friends are at altering camera snaps?

Boss man comes up with this story about a red headed girl and kids running about in ninja gear but it sounds just silly. Dad's version sounds much better especially as some of it's actually true. Everybody knows that he suddenly got accused of leaking secret information and he now gets to tell a lot of important people how exactly he came across them.

Dad's got an even better memory than me and can still recite all of the names on the list he saw on the enemy computer. But this time he includes Mr Williamson's name explaining that initially he'd not mentioned it as it was just too ridiculous to think that his own boss could be a double agent.

He also mentioned the package Mr Williamson received from the dispatch rider containing what looked like a secret photo of Boss man and a scribbled note.

"We're being watched and our phones monitored. Assume all is known. Come get me, I have an escape route."

I figured that Mr W wouldn't have a clue what Boss man's writing looked like and had to assume the note was genuine. He couldn't phone to check so had to go and find out for himself. A clever trap for a clever spider even if Dad took all of the credit for dreaming up the plan and kept my name out of it.

As we started following Mr W's car, Dad phoned his secret friend telling him that he's spotted boss man and is following. The friend alerts the local police who get their people onto quick emergency standby.

It's amazing what you can achieve when you're a spy and start talking about terrorists.

As soon as we reached the house, Dad gave the location to his friend and the whole plan swung into action. Ok, we muddled up some of the facts but what with the various photos we took and the explanations, Mr Williamson has no way of getting around why he just happened to be found chatting to his sworn enemy.

As I said, none of this made the news and I only know about it because of Dad and because of our own secret involvement.

While things are being quietly sorted out I get to rejoin the girls and Keira back at school and Dad gets his old job back and then a promotion. He also gets the job of going through that list of names again and looking very closely at the activities of all involved. It seems that some of the so called friendly names on the list might not be so friendly as Mr W made out. It all ends up with more knocks on doors and more secret meetings with people who won't be going home for a few years. That's assuming they don't hang traitors any more.

Back at the flat, we're just getting back into the normal school routine when one morning we get a knock on the door.

"Who'd like to go home?" Dad asks.

That would be everyone.

Everyone except me perhaps as I'm not sure where home is these days what with Mum and Dad now being divorced, and me living with Keira and the girls since forever.

The school gets told that Naz and Red have gone back to whatever country they came from and that I've been sent to another school which isn't so focussed on dancing. With my lack of grace on show each morning in class, this is a realistic explanation.

We'll miss our new found friends but the girls can't wait to see their proper families again. Of course there's lots of tears, they are girls after all, but it's quite a happy event when they get home even if it is a bit of a surprise.

I've got an even bigger surprise waiting for me after we extract ourselves from the homecoming girls.

Dad takes me and Keira for a short ride in his car and starts chatting about his new job. It sounds really important but it does mean that he'll be able to spend more time at home with me and we can be a real family again.

We stop outside this posh house on the edge of town and Dad gets out of the car.

"Don't you want to see your new home Jamie?" he asks.

Inside, he sends me off exploring while Keira makes us all a cup of tea. How does she know where everything is?

And why are they smiling?

"I've got some good news and some bad news Jamie," says Dad when we're all sat around the table.

Before I get a chance to choose what I'd like to hear first, he carries on.

"The good news is that Keira's going to be staying with us for a while. For quite a long while I hope."

Ah, that's why they're holding hands.

"The bad news is that although you can go back to your old boxing club with Big Jay, Keira won't be able to train you for a while and I'm afraid we're going to have to stop being ninjas for a bit as well."

That's a shame but I suppose it's best we go quiet after all that excitement. Don't want anyone to come looking for some kids who might dress up in ninja gear.

"Keira's got some news of her own as well."

She hands me this blurry looking photograph of an alien in all greys and shadows.

Ok, what am I missing? They're both sitting there grinning at me and there's obviously something else they've not been telling me.

"Don't you want to say hello to your new baby sister Jamie?"

Oh!

The End

Peter Marney

About the author

Peter Marney lives by the sea, is just as bad at drawing as Jamie, and falls over if his socks don't have the right day of the week written on them.

On a more serious note, Peter has worked supporting children with reading difficulties and understands some of their problems. He is passionate about the importance of both reading and storytelling to the growing mind.

Peter Marney

The Red Sock Ninja Clan Adventures

Birth of a Ninja

Jamie's about to start another new school and has been told to stay out of trouble. Like that's going to happen!

It's not as if he wants to fight but you've got to help out if a girl's being picked on, right? Even if it does turn out that she's the best fighter in the school and laughs at your odd socks.

Follow Jamie as he makes friends, sorts out a big problem at his school, and discovers that his weird new babysitter knows secret ninja skills.

Hide and Seek

Find out why Jamie hates dogs and why he's hiding in a school cupboard in the dark. Has it got something to do with Keira's new training games for the Red Sock Ninjas?

The Mystery Intruder

Someone is playing in school after dark and it's not just the Red Sock Ninjas. Maybe Harry knows who it is but he's not talking so Jamie will have to find another way to solve this mystery.

The Mighty Porcupine

What do you do when your enemy is too powerful to fight? Has somebody finally beaten the Red Sock Ninjas?

The Mystery Troublemakers

Someone wants to get Jamie's new youth club into trouble but why?

Maybe the Red Sock Ninjas can find the answer by climbing rooftops or will it just get them into more trouble?

Statty Sticks

Why is Jamie being attacked by a small girl who isn't Red and why does he get the feeling that someone is spying on him?

Has it got anything to do with why his school is in danger and how numbers can lie?

Enemies and Friends

Why has Jamie got a new uncle and why does everyone end up hiding in bushes?

Have the Red Sock Ninjas now found too big a porcupine and will it spell disaster for their future together?

Run Away Success

Where do you run to when everything goes wrong? That's the latest problem for the Red Sock Ninjas and this time Wally isn't around to mastermind the plan.

With the enemy closing in for capture, the friends must split up and disappear. Is this the end of the Clan or the beginning of a whole new experience for Jamie?

Rise and Shine

Why does going to the library get Jamie into a fight and what's that got to do with Keira's plan for getting rid of him?

Helping to put on a show with Miss G was difficult enough without guess who turning up. Yet again the Red Socks must use their skills to save the day and the show.

Rabbits and Spiders

Has Red set up Jamie on a date with Dog Girl? If so, why is he now running around in circles? Maybe it's got something to do with the fact that the enemy have at last found them again.

The Red Sock Ninjas must use all of their skills in this last adventure if they are to escape and live happily ever after.

Printed in Great Britain
by Amazon

43049192R00073